ESCAPE
FROM
PLANET
YASTOL

WAY-
TOO-REAL
ALIENS!

#1

ESCAPE
FROM
PLANET
YASTOL

PAMELA F. SERVICE · ILLUSTRATIONS BY MIKE GORMAN

darbycreek

MINNEAPOLIS

Darby Creek
A division of Lerner Publishing Group, Inc.
241 First Avenue North
Minneapolis, MN 55401 U.S.A.

Website address: www.lernerbooks.com

Main body text set in ITC Officina Sans Std Book 12/18
Typeface provided by International Typeface Corp

Library of Congress Cataloging-in-Publication Data

Service, Pamela F.
     Escape from planet Yastol / by Pamela F. Service ; illustrated by Mike Gorman.
        p.   cm. — (Way-too-real aliens ; #1)
     Summary: Eleven-year-old Joshua Higgins' prize-winning science fiction novel draws
   the attention of sinister blue aliens who capture Josh and his sister Maggie and take
   them to the planet Yastrol, the setting of his novel.
     ISBN: 978-0-7613-7918-8 (trade hard cover : alk. paper)
     [1. Extraterrestrial beings—Fiction. 2. Kidnapping--Fiction. 3. Authorship--Fiction.
   4. Books and reading—Fiction. 5. Brothers and sisters--Fiction. 6. Science fiction.] I.
   Gorman, Mike, ill. II. Title.
   PZ7.S4885Esc 2011
   [Fic]—dc22   2010049235

Manufactured in the United States of America
1 – SB – 7/15/11

FOR DOUG AND CAROL

-P.S.

TO JAY JACK AND ALL MY FAMILY
AT THE ACADEMY FOR INSPIRING
ME TO PUSH MYSELF FARTHER
THAN I IMAGINED POSSIBLE.

-M.G.

CHAPTER ONE
BLUE GUYS

Breathing hard, Prince Izor stopped to listen. The boots of Gorku's evil guards sounded on the stone steps behind him. Izor sped down the remaining stairs, his wavering torch casting wild shadows on the walls.

At the base of the steps he halted. Three warrior priests stood before him, purple hoods hiding their faces, gleaming swords in their hands. With a yell, Izor hurled his torch at them and leapt for the rafters above their heads. He swung himself up and, like a tight-rope walker, ran along the beam until he plunged onto a windowsill in the stone wall.

Teetering on the narrow ledge, Izor gazed in horror at the rocky valley below. Spears clanged against the stone beside him.

With a happy sigh, I slammed the book shut. Well, it wasn't really a slam—more of a *slup*. But my book was still a book!

I looked around the bookstore to see if anyone might have noticed me reading. Then I could walk over, casually praise the book and urge them to buy it. Okay, so I'm shameless.

But nobody was about. I put the book back on the shelf with the others and happily polished the sign. "*Danger on Yastol*, by Joshua P. Higgins, last year's winner of County School's annual Young Author Book Award."

Sure, it wasn't as thick and slick as those science fiction books on the rack behind me. But this was only the beginning! Someday I'd have a whole bunch of real books listed under my name, like those Famous Authors the school sometimes brought in to talk to us. Someday I would be the Famous Author wowing the kids.

I walked out of the bookshop into the mall's main plaza. Instantly my happiness shriveled. Bert Claypool and his gang of bullies were lounging on the benches by the potted trees. Bert grinned right at me.

"Joshua P. Higgins, King of the Bookworms. Every teacher's favorite."

I threw him a casual nod and pretended to look around for someplace else I had to be. Too late.

"Picking up your cut from those so-called books?"

"N . . . no. I don't get a cut. The money goes to covering the costs of the contest and the printing."

"What a success story!" Bert looked at the others. He had such a snotty grin on his face that I wanted to thump him. Except I'd get majorly thumped in return. "Don't we all wish we could rake in major bucks like that?"

Then he got right in my face. He'd been eating something with lots of garlic. "This junk you write will get you nothing. I'll be making millions as a pro quarterback while you're living on park benches, surrounded by stacks of your 'award-winning' books."

"Hey, bug off, slug face!" A voice shrilled behind him.

I looked and wished I could disappear. Just what my wimp image needed: kid sister Maggie, charging to the rescue.

Hands on her hips, she glared up at Bert. "You and your goons are just jealous because you don't have a creative thought between you. Josh will be on every talk show in the country while you're pushing brooms at some sports bar. Get off his case!"

Bert smirked. "Writers must be worse wimps than I thought. They've got to have little girls stand up for them." He turned to his gang. "Come on, guys. These two are a waste of air."

I watched them drift into the mall crowd. Then I turned on Maggie. "Let's get this straight, sis. You are my baby sister, not babysitter."

"Well, if you can't take care of yourself at age eleven, then someone's got to. Even if it's a ten year old. Jeez, Josh.

How come you can write about big brave heroes but can't act like one? I mean, it isn't like you have to punch the guy out. You just have to act like you could."

I tried for a snort. It was a pretty good one. Except I actually sprayed a little snot. "Acting! Pretending you're something you're not. No thanks. I'm heading home to do some writing."

I stomped out of the mall, feeling like a cartoon character—so angry that smoke ought to have been pouring out of my ears. I tried hard not to think about what Maggie had just said. But her words kept knocking around in my head anyway. Was that really why I wrote about big, brave heroes? Because I didn't have it in me to be one myself?

I took a deep breath, scowled back at Maggie, and stalked across the parking lot. I slipped around a sagging stretch of fence and headed off though the woods. The sharp early-spring air cooled my red face a little, but my thoughts were still superheated. So what if I was a major wimp? I'd just live with it. That was better than not admitting what I was and play acting all the time— like Maggie.

I heard her behind me, trudging through fallen twigs

and soggy leaves and babbling about her latest acting project. I wondered what I'd do if she was being bullied. I kicked at a pine cone. Probably I'd just slip away and let her act her way out of it.

She certainly seemed to be in her play acting world now. I hadn't been listening to her, but she hurried along to get me up to date. "Shakespeare is cool, except he's got too many weird words. We had to make some cuts, but it still should be great. Scenes from *A Midsummer Night's Dream*. Awesome. Tiffany and Melanie and I are doing all the parts, unless we can get some others to join us. I don't suppose you want to do a part?"

I nearly choked. "No way! Acting's a waste of time for someone like me. Actors are nothing without writers."

"Well, the least you could do is use your famous writing talent to write us a play. We wouldn't have to cut so much."

"I've got to get on with my new book for this year's contest. The deadline's getting close."

The grey winter woods around us were dotted with green. Curled young ferns and blades of grass poked through the mulch of old fallen leaves. Among all the grey and green, I thought I caught a glimpse of blue.

I stopped and glanced around. Nothing. I started up again, then quickly looked to my left. Gone. But I was sure I had seen something.

"What's the matter?" Maggie asked, stopping beside me.

"Nothing. Uh . . . were Bert and his gang wearing blue?"

"Blue? Maybe a couple were. You think they're following us or something?"

I couldn't admit it, but that was exactly what I was thinking. "Nah. Just thought I saw something. Come on."

The woods gave way to a wide clearing where trees had been ripped up for a new housing development. At the far end of the bare patch, a truck spun its wheels in the reddish mud. A yellow bulldozer pushed more tree trunks and dirt into a pile. I set off across the space and then spun around again. Once again something caught my eye. It hadn't looked like Bert's bullies.

"I saw it too," Maggie whispered. "Something bluish."

"Blue like police, maybe?"

"Get real. Why would police follow us?"

I thought over all the wrong things I'd done that

week. Telling jokes about our cranky principal, spending my lunch money on books, sneaking down to see a movie on TV after bedtime. Hardly police stuff. "It's probably just some other kids walking home from the mall."

"So why are they hiding?"

I shrugged. "Maybe they're pretending they're spies or something. You should know about that sort of thing, Miss Actress."

Determined to ignore anything blue, I cut through the next strip of woods and scrambled up onto the old railroad track. I strode between the wooden ties, looking for loose iron spikes to add to my collection.

"Josh," Maggie whispered. "Blue guys on the right."

Down the embankment, I saw a hint of blue disappear behind the rusty heap of a junked car. Okay, I was officially freaked out. But I wasn't going to let them know that, whoever they were.

"So, slowpoke," I said very loudly to Maggie, "how about a race? First one home gets the rest of the chocolate chip cookies."

Maggie burst along the track before I'd even shut my mouth. In the end, we hit the screen door at the same time and shared the cookies. Then Maggie went up to the attic to search for costumes for her play, and I headed up to my room to write. Our parents weren't home yet, so we had at least an hour until dinner.

I sat at my desk, thinking about this year's contest. Miss Jordan said they'd be expecting another award-winning piece from me. I stared at my computer's blank screen. No ideas sprang out of it. Should I do a sequel to *Danger on Yastol*? No, something new. But what? I got up and peered out the window. Was that a flicker of blue at the end of the garden? Maybe I should write about blue guys who flit in and out of sight.

I shook my head and pulled the curtains closed. I had a creepy feeling I wouldn't like the way that story went.

CHAPTER TWO
LATE-WINTER NIGHT'S BAD DREAM

A good night's sleep kind of puts creepy things in their place. The next morning, the blue guys were as easy to forget as last week's stomachache. But one problem still hung around: I needed a story idea. The need ate at me all through Saturday breakfast and chores. As soon as I could, I went to my room, turned my back on the sunny day at the window, and sat down at my computer.

Nothing. Absolutely nothing came to me.

Writer's block sat on my chest like a very heavy cat. I got up and paced around the room. The last Famous Author who spoke at our school had said that the best way to get rid of writer's block was to do something else. Clean your room maybe, or take a walk. No choice there.

Spring was even more sprung that morning than it had been the day before. Green buds and little purple flowers were popping up everywhere. I headed for the woods.

The bulldozers weren't working that day, and all I could hear were birds chuckling to themselves. Then something else. From down in the hollow I heard voices. I stopped dead. *Blue guys?* I fought off an urge to run the other way and crept closer.

Crouching behind a mossy log, I peered into a clearing. Maggie and her friends were practicing their scenes from *A Midsummer Night's Dream.*

Chuckling at myself, I watched. Tall, skinny Melinda wore a beach towel cape and a Robin Hood-looking hat.

She stepped from behind a bush and pointed a stick dramatically at Tiffany. "Ill met by moonlight, proud Titania."

I guess Tiffany was supposed to be this Titania person. She was wearing a way-too-big floaty nightgown. Prancing forward, she sneered. "What, jealous Oberon? Fairies, skip hence. I have forsworn his company."

Maggie, who had been watching from her seat on a stump, jumped up and waved some papers. "Wait a minute, guys. Melinda, you can't play Oberon, because you also play Nick Bottom. They're both in the same scene later."

"We've all got too many parts," Melinda complained. "We'll just have to let more kids in on this."

"Okay," Maggie agreed. "We'll ask Liz and Jenny on Monday."

"Not Liz!" Tiffany wailed. "She's so bossy. She'll want to run everything."

Maggie nodded. "Okay. Paula then. But let's practice that scene between Puck and the chief fairy. As Puck I say, 'Then speakest thou aright. I am that merry wanderer of the night.' And then I run off and jump over something like, say, that mossy log over there."

She started to skip right toward me. I flattened myself like a slug. No good. She jumped onto the log, right above me.

"Yikes!" she cried

"What's the matter?" Tiffany and Melinda called together.

"I've found a spy!" She looked down at me with a really wicked smile. "No, better yet. I've found someone to play Oberon."

"No way!" I yelled jumping to my feet. "I *don't like* acting."

"And I don't like people spying. We need an Oberon— just for this rehearsal." She lowered her voice. "And if you don't do it, I'll tell Melinda, Tiffany, and everybody how you freaked out yesterday at a troop of Cub Scouts."

She had me, and she knew it. I tromped after her into the clearing, trying to think of ways to get back at her. She threw me a paper-clipped wad of typed sheets.

"Your script," she said pointing to a thorny bush. "You stand over there and step out from the bush when I tell you and read your lines."

Grudgingly, I did as she ordered and glowered at the script until she pointed at me like some grand orchestra director. I stepped forward and read the lines in as flat a voice as I could.

"Ill met by moonlight, proud Titania."

"What, jealous Oberon?" Tiffany said with a haughty flip of her nightgown. "Fairies, skip hence. I have forsworn his company."

"Tarry, rash wonton," I read. "Am I not thy lord?"

"Not *wonton*!" Maggie yelled. "That's something you eat in a Chinese restaurant. It's *wanton*. A bad woman.

How come if you write words so well, you can't speak them?"

I threw down the script. "Because it's a waste of my talent. Writing takes *skill*."

Melinda sniffed and snatched off her towel cape. "Well, it's a waste of *my* talent to rehearse with this oaf. Besides, I told my mom I'd come home about now."

"Me too," Tiffany added, following Melinda out of the clearing. "We'll see if we can't recruit some *real* talent Monday. Even Liz would be better than him."

That left me and Maggie in the clearing. She stood, hands on hips, glowering at me. "The only talent you have, Joshua P. Higgins, is for spoiling other people's fun. And you're sure no Shakespeare. Nobody's going to be acting your stuff four hundred years from now."

"Hah! If Shakespeare had known that a bunch of dweebs like you would be acting his plays, he wouldn't have bothered writing them."

Maggie crossed her arms. "That shows just how much you . . ."

"Shhh!" I put my argument with Maggie on hold. A sudden movement in the woods had snatched my attention. "The blue guys."

Maggie rolled her eyes. She's really good at that. "You think I'll fall for that? Beware the big bad Cub Scouts."

I didn't know what the creatures were that were coming from the woods, but they were not Cub Scouts. Grabbing Maggie's hand, I dragged her out of the clearing. She squawked, looked behind us, and went silent. I didn't have to drag her anymore.

We crashed through the edge of the woods, burst into the open, and ran across the bare construction site. I guess *running* isn't the word. We began to slip and slide in the red mud. I glanced behind me. The blue guys weren't having much trouble. They were gaining. Before we passed the yellow bulldozer they had us surrounded.

For the first time, I got a good look at them. I wished I hadn't.

They were tall, flat, and faceless, sort of like big sticks of gum—blue gum. The tops of their heads were fluttering strips. Other strips flapped at the ends of their noodly arms and legs. The creatures were so skinny that when they turned sideways, they almost disappeared. I couldn't read their expressions, but nothing about them seemed friendly.

One of the blue guys wiggled the strips at the top of its head. A thin, grating sound filled the air. *Was that talking?* Two others leapt forward and stuffed what looked like hairnets on top of my and Maggie's heads. I struggled to yank mine off until I noticed that the blue guys' odd sounds had become chirpy English. *The nets must be translator things*, I realized. I stopped tugging.

"Good," one of them chirped. "Intelligent enough not

to fight. You. Taller one. You are the Joshua P. Higgins. Correct?"

For a moment, I just stared, trying to force sound out past the fear in my throat. "Yes," I finally managed.

"Author of *Danger on Yastol*?"

"What? You mean . . . Well, sure, I wrote it." I felt like giggling wildly. What were these guys, book critics? Fans?

"Good. You will take us there."

"Where?"

This thing is getting majorly weird, I thought. "You want to go to the bookstore? Buy a copy?"

"Have copies. You take us to Yastol."

I laughed. "You've got to be kidding. That's not a real place. I just made it up."

The creature grunted. "Not intelligent after all. You humans are actualizers. You can tune in to other worlds. One of the few species in the universe. You write about them in what you call fiction."

"Wait a minute!" Maggie interrupted, disbelief on her face. "You mean all these books and stories people write . . . they're just describing the way things are someplace else?"

"Correct. What are you, shorter person? Does Joshua P. Higgins need you for his work?"

"What? Oh sure. I'm his critic. He can't write anything without me telling him where it stinks."

"I do not understand. But will accept. You come too . . ."

I'd had enough craziness. "Hold on a minute. We're not going anywhere with you guys, real or made-up. We're going home."

"Perhaps. But first you go to Yastol." The creature raised a noodle arm and threw me a silver circlet. Instinctively I caught it. It looked like a crown for a school play—shiny, with three blue glass jewels set in the front.

"Put on head," the creature rasped at me.

"Why?"

"Must explain basics. Most species in universe not like you humans. Cannot see other worlds in our minds. Do not have fiction."

"I'm sorry to hear that," I said as I tried to hand back the circlet. "Sounds pretty boring. But really, I've got a lot of homework to do. I don't have time to write you up something just now."

"Do not talk!" the blue guy snapped. "We do not require

anything new. It is *Danger on Yastol* that interests us. Read thousands of human stories. Look for something of use to us. You describe a mine that has in it smooth purple stone flecked with silver: *aafth*."

The word didn't translate. It sounded like the speaker had been punched in the stomach.

The guy continued. "We need aafth for our weapons. For our spaceships. It is rare in the known worlds. But there are many worlds in the universe. You described a world where there is much of it. Enough to give us power to conquer the galaxy."

"How nice for you," I muttered. I figured this had to be some kind of hoax. Could Bert be behind it, trying to make more fun of me and my book? How had he managed the effects? I decided to play along a bit longer and then split.

"But sorry, I really can't help you. I mean, as far as I knew, I'd just made the place up. I couldn't possibly get you there."

"Incorrect," a second blue guy said, wobbling forward. "You humans may be actualizers. But you are very stupid with machines. *We* excel at machines. We have made a device to link into an actualizer's brain. To take him and others to place described."

"Well, that sure sounds great," Maggie piped up. "But I read that book of his too, even before he finished it. Believe me, Yastol isn't the sort of place you want to visit. All dry and full of scary stuff. So forget about it, and we'll just go home."

"Incorrect!" the lead guy snapped as he stepped forward.

That was it. I grabbed Maggie's hand and we dashed away. As we passed the bulldozer, I tossed the silver circlet aside. Veering around the machine, I looked back and saw a blue guy scoop up the circlet and jam the end of a high-tech-looking staff into the blue jewels. Then I concentrated on running. But the gooey red mud slowed us down. It clung to our feet in messy clumps.

Beside me, Maggie yelped as the mud grabbed hold of one of her shoes. I stopped to help her tug free.

A floppy blue hand grabbed my arm. Someone jammed the silver circlet on my head. I fought to pull away but lost my balance. I teetered on the edge of a rain-filled pit left by the bulldozer. Still gripping Maggie's hand, I fell toward the red earth and muddy water.

When I landed, the earth underneath me was purple and there was no water in sight.

CHAPTER THREE
JUST AS IMAGINED

Maggie and I huddled on the dry ground, surrounded by five blue guys. You'd think they'd be hard to ignore. But for a moment, I did. I stared at the landscape beyond them.

The purple ridge we were crouched on dipped into a vast purple desert. Here and there, spires and mesas of blue, red, and violet poked up in the distance. A painfully bright silver sun lit up the pale lavender sky.

"Yastol," I whispered as I slowly stood up. "Just as I imagined it."

Beside me, Maggie was on her feet too, fanning herself with a hand to fight the hot dry air. "Josh, couldn't you have imagined some place with lots of water and cool trees while you were at it?"

"Foolish one." A blue guy unplugged the shiny staff

31

from the circlet and yanked both from my head. "If he had, it would have been a different world he saw. Of no use to us. It is Yastol and its aafth that we want. Hurry, humans. We must be sure that all is as we need it at the mines."

They began slapping us with their noodle arms, herding me and Maggie toward a dark blue peak. I guess I should have been a lot more scared than I was, but I just kept looking in awe at the world around me, muttering at the wonders of this or that. Beside me, Maggie muttered more angry things.

Finally, she turned to one of our captors. "Once you've found your stupid rocks, will you send us home?"

"The coordinates for this planet and the route to and from are now fixed in the circlet," one answered. "If our examination shows that you have indeed brought us to the correct aafth-rich world, we will have no more need of you."

"That's not quite what I asked," Maggie said under her breath.

The blue guy's words didn't quite sink in. I was still too wrapped up in seeing "my" world unfold. "It's incredible. Look at those yellow towers way off in the distance.

Like a sparkling sand castle. Just like I wrote! That must be Jiz Tah—the capital where Prince Izor lives!"

"Yeah, I know," Maggie grumbled. "Along with King and Queen What's-Their-Names. Will you stop playing tourist for a minute and figure out how we're going to get out of this?"

"But this is so cool. I mean, some of the things I just sketchily described so I could get on with the story. But here all the details are filled in. This place is really real, not just something that hangs out in my mind. It's so awesome!"

Maggie snorted. "About as awesome as getting killed. Real or made-up, I bet we'll be just as dead."

That got through to me. I looked back to where the blue guys were walking behind us, jabbering among themselves. "We'll make it out. That guy said they'd send us back once we checked out the mines."

"Incorrect," Maggie said in a perfect imitation of their flat tones. I hate to admit it, but she really is a good actress. "They said they wouldn't need us after that."

"Oh. Yeah." Cold fear dribbled over my excitement. "Those black tubes they're carrying. Do you think they're weapons?"

"How would I know?" she snapped. "I didn't write a

story about these freaks!"

"Neither did I!" I snapped back. "The Yastoli look like people, only they're orange and have different shades of pink hair. I'm not sick enough to think up walking sticks of blue gum."

We trudged through the heat in silence. The blue mountain way ahead of us cast the only shade for miles. Sure, I'd written about that mountain and all, but Maggie was right. I had to stop being a tourist and come up with some way to get us out of here. One that didn't involve getting killed.

The air around us shimmered in the heat. Squinting through it, I could see a dark patch at the mountain's base. The mine entrance. Shapes that looked like round boulders were clustered outside. The huts of workers who tried to make a living scraping leftover gold out of the abandoned mine. Maybe they could help us somehow.

As we drew closer, several orange people stepped out of their huts and pointed towards us. A party of blue guys and humans, we must have looked pretty strange to them. Still, I was getting excited about meeting my first real Yastoli. I hoped that the translator nets worked on other species as well.

A blue guy growled behind us. I turned to see one of

them raise a black tube. It fired a spray of white light toward the huts with a hiss. The huts and people turned a glowing white and melted like wax.

Stunned, I yelled, "You can't do that! They're people. You can't go around killing people like that."

"They are only natives," the weapon-shooter said flatly. "We are here for planet's minerals. Natives get in the way."

A blue guy prodded me and Maggie forward, past the smoking patch of ground. I felt sick. Even if I hadn't really created them, the Yastoli were special to me. I'd just seen a bunch killed like they were ants. And I don't even like to see ants killed.

"Guess that proves it," Maggie whispered shakily. "These are not nice guys. Not likely to say 'thanks so much' and send us home."

I nodded, still quivering inside. "We'll get away soon. Maybe while they're looking around the mine."

Maggie frowned. "How come if this mine is abandoned, it still has what these guys want?"

"These mines were dug for gold," I told her. "I thought I just made up the purple stone with silver flecks to sound pretty. Maybe if I'd described green stone with red flecks, I'd have been talking about another world or another dimension or something. And these guys would have left us alone."

Maggie shook her head. "Or maybe there's another bunch of nasties looking for green stone with red flecks." She sighed. "I knew writing stories was a dumb idea."

The mine entrance loomed before us like a huge open mouth. Maggie and I slowed to a halt, staring into the gloom. Two swift swats from blue guys and we stumbled inside.

It was more than dark in there—it was cool. That felt really good after the blazing heat outside. One of our captors raised a metal cube that started glowing like a flashlight. The ceiling of the mine was maybe ten feet high. In the light it looked like a deep purple sky sparkling with thousands of silver stars.

"Wealth!" one of the blue guys cried. "Riches! All that aafth. Ten planets' worth, right here. We will rule the galaxy!"

They were all so excited about the aafth that they seemed to have forgotten us completely. Unfortunately they stood between us and the mine entrance. But the light seeping in from the front showed several tunnels snaking off into the darkness. Maggie and I were inching toward the nearest one when one blue guy turned sharply toward us. "Yes, this is the right place," he chuckled. "We are finished with you now. Go."

One floppy hand held the silver circlet. The other held a black metal tube. That was the one he pointed toward us.

I froze. Maggie squealed. With wide eyes, she pointed wildly behind the blue guys. "What's that?"

They all spun around. In a flash, I leapt forward and snatched the circlet. We both charged down the tunnel.

"That's the oldest trick in the book," I called as we ran.

Maggie giggled. "Guess they haven't read that book."

As we sped away from the entrance, I realized the tunnel wasn't pitch black. Silver flecks in the aafth sparkled in the walls, floor, and ceiling. They gave off a faint glow, enough to keep us from running into walls as the tunnel twisted and turned. Still, we stumbled over the uneven floor. We would have slowed down, but we could hear the swishing, flapping sound of running blue guys not far behind us.

The tunnel suddenly branched into three pathways. We veered into one and kept running. Then that tunnel branched into seven. We chose the third from the left at random and raced down it.

"You know," Maggie panted after a while, "we're totally lost."

"Better than being melted," I answered. But I wasn't totally sure of that. I tried to remember what I had said about these tunnels. Not much. But I had mentioned that the miners were afraid of some of them. Afraid of the "mine beasts." That's all I'd said. I hadn't even described these beasts. Now I wished I'd said they were sweet little balls of fur who wouldn't hurt a gnat.

They weren't.

CHAPTER FOUR
FROM FRYING PAN TO FIRE

"Gak!" I managed to croak as Maggie and I stumbled to a halt. Ahead, four orange eyes, large as headlights, glowed high up in the dark. Rumbling filled the tunnel like an oncoming train. I would have preferred a train. The rocks' faint light glinted off a large set of pointy teeth below the three eyes. The stench of rotten meat wafted up the tunnel.

"Gak!" came the translated cry from behind us as five blue guys skidded to a halt.

The beast lowered its glowing eyes and crouched down, preparing to pounce.

Maggie clutched my hand. "What do we do?"

"Duck!"

Just as the beast sprang, we crouched down. Its claws and its stink sailed by inches above us. The rumbling turned into a roar, followed by a horrible scream. Leaping to our feet, we ran.

We pelted down tunnel after tunnel with no idea where we were going—except to get away from where we had been. Finally, the only sounds we heard came from our own terrified feet. Exhausted, we sank to the cold stone floor.

"We are so totally lost," Maggie moaned.

I tried to think up something encouraging to say. I didn't do too well. "Well, if we don't know where we are, neither do they."

"Great. And if that four-eyed stink bomb didn't poison itself eating blue guys, it could be stalking us now."

I forced myself up on my quivering legs. "Right. So let's keep moving. Some of these tunnels have got to lead to the outside. I think."

"Great. He thinks." Maggie got up and continued walking beside me. "I wish he'd thought better of writing this story," she mumbled. "Now, we'll wander for days until we die because we haven't anything to eat or because something eats us, and we'll never get home, never see our parents, and I'll never get to do my scenes from *Midsummer Night's Dream*!"

Maggie grumbled on until I guess her throat got too dry. I didn't bother getting annoyed. Having an annoying little sister was nothing new. At least I wasn't alone in this endless dark maze.

Dark? I squinted ahead. Was it looking a little greyer down there?

We rushed forward. An exit! Fresh air! At last we stood happily blinking in the light, arms outstretched in the hot, dry wind. The silver sun hung low in the sky. Inky shadows spilled over the purple landscape. Never when I was writing about this world did I believe it could be as beautiful as it was then.

"We made it! We made it!" Maggie sang as she spun around. She turned to me, then jumped back and pointed dramatically at my shoulder. "What's red with pink spots and lots of legs?"

"Come off it," I groaned. "Next you'll say 'I don't know either, but there's one on your shoulder.' That's the second-oldest trick in the book."

She shrugged. "Maybe so, but there's still one on your shoulder."

I started laughing, then felt a funny itching on my shoulder. I tried not to look. The itching got worse. I looked.

"Gak!"

It was red with pink spots and lots of legs. It also had a lot of teeth, which is why I didn't just flick it off. It had those teeth, a couple of eyes on short stalks, and a six-inch-long, sausage-shaped body. It blinked at me, then settled down to scratch itself with a couple of its many legs.

"Got a lot of legs, hasn't it?" Maggie said.

"Sure does," I said, trying to sound calm and ignore her smug smile. "And a lot of fleas, by the look of it."

"Great. The leggy fleabag is all yours." Maggie shrugged. "So what do we do now, Great Author?"

Remembering the mine beast behind us, I led us further from the tunnel opening. I struggled to think up an answer. "Well, now we've got the circlet back," I said, patting my shirt where I'd stuffed the thing. "But if it's got information stored in it like the blue guys said, they probably need it to get home or ship out the aafth or something. So they might still be after us. If they weren't all eaten."

"Right. So let's go home before they find us." Maggie snatched the thing out from under my shirt and jammed it on my head. "We should have tried this earlier! Go on, think about home."

I wasn't sure that was how this worked, but it was worth a try. Squinching my eyes closed, I thought about my bedroom. I thought about the bookstore in the mall. I even thought about the clearing in the woods where Maggie rehearsed plays. Nothing happened.

Sighing, I took off the circlet and stuffed it carefully back under my shirt. "No good. Maybe we need the long staff thing that they hooked into it."

"And they've got that," Maggie groaned. "So we need to find them too. They couldn't have all been eaten by that beast. Probably some of them used a melting gun and got away."

My shoulder itched. I'd almost forgotten about my spotted passenger. I looked to see it licking its paws like a cat. It grinned at me with its mouthful of sharp teeth, then strolled down my arm and slipped into my pocket. I shuddered and looked out at the landscape.

"I wish I knew this place better. I mean, Miss Jordan may be a good English teacher when it comes to writing fiction, but she's lousy when it comes to describing reality. She kept saying, 'Don't put in details you don't need for your story.' But how about details you may need to keep alive? I sure wish I'd described every inch of this place."

"Okay, brilliant author," Maggie snapped, "there's got to be some clue. Does the sun set in the west here like it does at home?"

I squinted at the silvery sun, now much closer to the

horizon. "Yes, I think I said it did. Ah! Then if that's west, north is to our right. And I said the main mine entrance was on the north side of the mountain!"

We headed off in that direction, scrambling over rocks that had once tumbled off the mountain. It would have been nice if we'd run into a pond or stream or something. My mouth felt like it was coated with sawdust. But I'd said this place was a desert. And I was so right.

I was just crawling over yet another boulder when I grabbed Maggie and scrunched down. "Blue guys ahead," I whispered. I risked a peek through a crack in the rock. "They're going in and out of the mine. Four of them. The mine beast seems to have just picked off one." I shuddered, remembering that horrible scream.

Maggie found another gap and peered through. "The taller one's carrying the staff. What'll we do?"

"Wait for a chance to grab it, I guess." Not a great plan, but I didn't have any of those.

After a long while staring through air wiggling with heat, we saw the taller blue guy put down everything he was carrying, including the staff, to help carry out a large slab of purple stone. Like a lizard, I began inching forward.

Something clamped over my mouth and swept me into the air. Thrashing and flipping about, I expected to see a blank blue face staring into mine. Instead, the face was orange.

A deep orange, topped with day-glo pink hair. The man's beard and moustache were just as pink. One ear was pierced with three green earrings. I groaned. A Yastoli slave trader.

He crammed a dirty rag in my mouth and flipped me

over his shoulder like a sack of laundry. As we jogged away from the mountain, I looked back to see another Yastoli carrying Maggie. But bouncing upside down, it was hard to focus on anything, or even think. I had to close my eyes and just focus on not getting sick.

At last, the jogging stopped. I slid open my eyes. We were standing on a ridge. The desert floor below folded into a narrow valley. A bunch of Yastoli were camped down there, along with a small herd of grey-green riding beasts.

"These two will bring a good reward," the guy carrying me chuckled as he started down the slope. At least the translator net seemed to work on these guys too. *Maybe we can talk our way out of this*, I thought.

That hope shriveled as we were dropped at the feet of a very fat Yastoli in a glowing green robe.

"O great Knishak," my captor crowed, "we found these two by the old mines. See their unusual color. They should bring a good price."

Maggie dropped beside me, and someone yanked off our gags. I could only groan. I had written about Knishak. A major villain who terrorized half the planet. He looked even nastier than I'd said. Clumps of dirt clung to his knotty pink beard. His paunch strained against a golden sash that also held a wicked-looking curved dagger. If only I could have said he was a real sweetie with a heart of gold!

Knishak grunted and poked us with his jeweled walking stick. "Small and puny. But they'll grow—if they survive. Throw them in with the other young one."

Maggie jumped up. "You bully! You can't just . . ." Knishak's walking stick struck her sharply in the face. She staggered back, clutching her cheek.

Without thinking, I jumped forward and smacked the stick out of the slaver chief's hand. "Leave my sister alone, you lard bucket! We are not your slaves!"

Knishak's jowly face turned an even deeper orange. His mouth slid into a thin smile. "They bring a better price when they still have some spirit. We'll leave it to their new masters to beat it out of them. Take them away!"

The traders herded us through a crowd of camping Yastoli slaves. Except for the obvious guards, they were a miserable-looking group, dirty and ragged, huddled together out in the open. No locks or chains—maybe fear of the slavers was enough to keep them contained. The traders shoved us against a pile of brown rags at the crowd's edge. Maggie shivered like a lost puppy beside me. She dabbed an old tissue against the bloody scratch on her cheek.

Awkwardly, I put an arm around her. "Are you hurt bad?"

She shook her head and then blew her nose on the crumpled tissue. "Not much. It really scared me, though, when you jumped him like that. That was awfully brave, Josh." She grinned. "Stupid, but brave. I guess you don't just write about heroes, after all."

"Nah, I was just mad. A real brave hero-type wouldn't have let himself get caught by those goons in the first place."

Just then, the pile of rags beside us stirred. A face peered out at us: orange, with purpley-pink hair.

I gasped. "Prince Izor!" Exactly as I'd imagined him.

"Hush!" the boy lunged forward, clapping a hand over my mouth. "The slavers mustn't know who I am."

We glanced around. A couple guards stood out of earshot, talking to each other. The other captives were some distance away, huddling close together against the cold of approaching night. Already the sun had slipped behind distant mountains. Chilly darkness was spreading like a stain.

We looked back at the prince, to find him staring at the two of us. "You know me," he said, "but who are you? You don't look like you're from around here."

I thought quickly. The Yastoli believe in magic, but not in people from other planets. Hearing that would totally freak him out . . .

I glanced warningly at Maggie. She nodded, stood up, and bowed dramatically. "O great prince, this is Josh the Oberon, master of many mystic arts.

I am Maggie the Puck, his assistant. We are, in fact, from distant . . . distant, eh . . ."

"Timthfar," I supplied. That was someplace I'd mentioned in the book as a little-known continent far to the south. The people there were supposed to be pretty strange.

"Ah," the prince said, nodding his head. "And the spirits sent you to rescue me?"

"Well, not . . ." I began, but Maggie jumped in again.

"Who can tell the way of the spirits? But tell us how you, the crown prince of Jiz Tah, happen to be captive here."

He frowned. Studying his face, I decided that orange wasn't too bad a color for skin. But the shocking pink hair was a bit much when you saw it for real.

"It's my own fault," the prince said gloomily. "After my run-ins with the priests of Nur and the Majawi pirates, my father practically locked me in the palace. He said he couldn't have the heir of Jiz Tah risking his life in more adventures—even if that heir had managed to defeat pirates and overthrow a wicked high priest. Finally I got so screaming bored, I snuck out of the palace dressed as a commoner. I was working on a farm when the slavers swooped down and captured us. Now I wish I'd stayed home and stayed bored. It beats being sold as a galley slave."

Huddled in his filthy blanket, Izor looked so miserable that I wanted to pat him on the back. But I wasn't sure you could do that with a prince. So I just smiled encouragingly. "Cheer up. I guess you can't be heroic all the time."

"Heroic?" he laughed grimly. "What's heroic about acting first and thinking later? I've been lucky up to now, but it looks like my luck has run out."

"No way!" I said. "Surely your father or Abem the Spy Master will be on your trail soon?"

He looked at me narrowly. "How do you know Abem the Spy Master? His very existence is secret."

"Josh the Oberon knows many things," Maggie said mysteriously. Then she grinned at me. "Go ahead, Great Oberon. Tell him some of the strange things you know."

I thought quickly, rummaging through the story details in my head. "I know that your favorite pajamas are blue-and-tan striped. . . and you hide candy in the dragon statue in your father's throne room. Oh yeah, and you think the cook's daughter is the cutest thing on two legs. Next to Princess Elya of Zog, that is."

Izor's mouth dropped open. "Wonderful! You are indeed magic workers."

"Not exactly. At least, I can't work magic to make these guards disappear. I just . . . know things."

Absently I started scratching an itch on my chest and brushed against something bumpy. Startled, I saw that the polka-dotted thing with lots of legs and teeth had crawled out of my pocket. "Oh, I forgot about Leggy here. What is this thing anyway, Izor?"

Eyes huge, he stared at me. "You are a most fortunate person, Josh the Oberon. That is a dit-dit. Very rare. They live in caves and become very attached to people—one way or another. Either they start eating the person right away, or they become very devoted pets."

I swallowed. "Oh. Just what I always wanted, a pet buzz saw."

"Well, I'll tell you what I want," Maggie interrupted. "I want to get away from here and find the blue guys before they find us. I mean, this Knishak is a real slime, but those guys melt people, for crying out loud!"

"What blue guys?" Izor began. Just then, a couple of guards stomped over and threw down ragged blankets, a loaf of bread, and a leather jug of water.

"Eat, slaves. Then stop jabbering and sleep. Tomorrow's trek is hard."

I looked at the meager meal. Maggie and I hadn't eaten since the breakfast Mom had fixed that morning. Suddenly, homesickness washed over me. I felt kind of like Dorothy—unhappy even in Oz. Heroic adventures were great on paper, but this was real. Deadly real. We could have gotten melted by the blue guys or stabbed by the boss slaver. Even my story's hero was trapped.

As I chewed my share of the stale bread and gulped dirty water, I was totally, one-hundred-percent miserable. Why hadn't I written a nice safe story about puppies or an ordinary schoolkid in an ordinary American town? It wouldn't have won any prizes, but it wouldn't have dumped us here either. Being a Famous Author certainly wasn't what it was cracked up to be.

CHAPTER FIVE
ESCAPE AND BETRAYAL

With the rocky ground beneath me and icy air all around, I shouldn't have slept. But, totally exhausted, I did. Until something in the middle of the night woke me up. Two of the planet's three reddish moons loomed high overhead. I'd described the moons as "pale tomatoes floating in a dark soup." Not all that poetic maybe, but there they were—it fit. But I had said nothing about this world's stars. Now I could see those too, cold and sharp, scattered over the black sky in strange patterns.

I strained my ears to try to find what had woken me.

There was the rustle of faint movement. Then I felt a dull poke in my ribs. Maggie raised her head from the ragged blanket next to mine. "Josh, let's try to get away," she whispered. "I know those guards are scary, but I really want to go home."

"Shh," Izor hissed from his own heap of rags. "I hear someone moving around out there."

Cautiously, I propped myself up on an elbow. I could see the dark-humped shapes of sleeping men and animals. Beyond them, tall rectangular shapes were moving. Someone cried out. Brilliant white light flashed across the camp.

"The blue guys!" I yelled over a rising flurry of screams. "Let's split! You too, Izor. You really don't want to meet these guys."

"Why? Haven't they come to free you with their magic weapons?"

"Being melted isn't the kind of freedom I'd like. Move!"

Crouching close to the ground, we scurried toward the edge of the camp. The guards who had encircled the camp were all caught up in the fray. Around us, the air filled with bright flashes, shouts, and the twang of Yastoli bows.

"Deliver us your human captives!" a blue guy cried.

The chaos helped our escape. Soon we reached the posts where the slavers' saddled animals were tied. We freed three, mounted up, and started galloping toward the western hills.

That makes it sound like a dashing escape. But I'm no horseback rider. And my beast was no horse. Scrambling onto its back was like climbing a slippery hippopotamus.

At least the saddle was like a bucket—once I'd wedged myself in, it was hard to fall out. I had no idea how to steer the thing, but my beast and Maggie's seemed happy to follow Izor's with no directions from us.

As we thudded away from the slaver camp, I looked in wonder at my mount. A cwoo, a real cwoo! I'd had fun with what I thought was making up a really outlandish riding animal. Now I was on one. It was leathery, fat, and the color of mildew, with a low, wide head, curly horns, and a wide mouth. But it had long, graceful legs like a deer, six of them.

"Where are we headed?" I called to Izor over the thudding of all those hooves.

"To the temple of Nur," he called back. "It's not far."

I thought a moment. "Then we'd better take the secret back way because of the hidden traps on the main road."

After a silence, the prince said, "You do know amazing things, secret things. But that way is safe now. Those traps were cleared after High Priest Gorku was overthrown."

We were all riding side by side now. Maggie joined in. "Yeah. Was I ever glad you beat that Gorku guy. He was a real nasty."

I could almost feel confusion radiating from the prince. But he rode on in silence. Good thing the Yastoli expect magic workers to be mysterious.

Ahead, the rosy moonlight showed a road rising toward a cluster of towers on a mountain peak. I'd described the temple of Nur as a massive and kind of scary place. But not as scary as where we'd left. Behind us, booms and flashes still came from the slavers' camp. I hoped that other captives got away in all the confusion. I also hoped that the blue guys hadn't noticed our escape. But in the bright double-moonlight, that didn't seem likely.

The moonlight gradually faded as dawn neared. By the time we reached the temple gate, the sky was a pale purple. Izor leapt off his steed and hammered on the heavy wooden door. "Open in the name of the king!" he shouted.

In moments, a sleepy-looking priest cracked open the door. He staggered back. "Prince Izor! Enter. I'll . . . I'll fetch the High Priest."

I tensed up, then remembered that this had to be a new high priest. The evil Gorku had been overthrown in chapter eleven.

The new guy turned out to be a little old man whose orange skin was as wrinkled as a month-old jack-o'-lantern. "O, great prince," he said, bowing so low that his pale pink beard swept the dust. "How may we serve you?"

"Your Graciousness, you may give me and my friends food and a place to rest. And you may also set guards on the walls and gate. There may be some. . . strange-looking, dangerous creatures following us." He shot me a questioning look.

I nodded. "Right, Your Graciousness. Tall blue ones. You couldn't miss them. Really bad business."

"Indeed," Izor continued. "And could you send a message bird to Jiz Tah? Tell my father that I am here."

"It shall be so, my prince," the old guy said, bowing again. "Brother Gom will take you to a room where you can rest and eat."

A younger priest stepped forward and pushed back his purple hood. I barely stifled my gasp. He sure looked like how I'd described Gom, the sneaky little assistant to the former High Priest Gorku. Surely Prince Izor wouldn't trust him. But then, Izor hadn't been in those scenes with Gom. So maybe he wouldn't know about him. And just maybe, with his former boss gone, Gom had reformed.

He certainly seemed eager to please. Smiling and bowing, he led us through a walled garden where a tinkling fountain rose from beds of softly-colored flowers. The air was heavy with perfume. After the bare desert, this place looked like paradise.

We walked through an arched doorway into a building made of pale blue stone. After climbing several flights of stairs, Gom showed us to a large room with fancy rugs scattered over the floor. Sunlight and an early morning breeze streamed in through arched windows. In a tiled side room, a sunken bathtub was already filled with steaming water. This wasn't part of the temple complex I'd described. But it sure looked good to me.

Brother Gom left us for a moment, then returned with a tray holding things to eat and drink. Really good-smelling things. He placed it on a low table and, walking backwards, bowed his way out and closed the door.

It didn't take the three of us long to plunk down and start stuffing our faces. The dit-dit circled my plate and peeped for its share. After gorging myself, I fed it slices of blue fruit and little honey cakes. Its sharp teeth ripped into everything like a paper shredder.

The smell of flowers rose from the garden below as the rising sun warmed the air. The sound of priests singing their prayers drifted up as well. Snuggling back into my pillow, I decided that maybe it wasn't so bad being in a story world. Thoughts of Gom kept eating at me, though.

Lazily, I gazed out the arched window at the cloudless lavender sky. A turquoise messenger bird took to the air on its flight to Jiz Tah, silver sunlight glinting on its wings.

A faint twang came from the garden below. An arrow shot after the bird like a missile. In a burst of feathers, the bird fell from the sky.

CHAPTER SIX

TEMPLE TREASON

"Izor!" I yelled, jumping up so fast I knocked Leggy into a bowl of pudding. "Someone just shot down your messenger bird!"

We rushed to the window—no sign of the archer. But looking beyond the temple walls, we glimpsed something else. Three distant blue figures marched steadily up the road.

"Are those your pursuers?" Izor asked.

I grunted. "Looks like them."

"But there're only three now," Maggie pointed out. "The slaver guards must have taken out one."

"What do they want with you?" Izor asked.

I looked at the prince. This was going to be hard to explain without totally freaking him out, but he needed to know the danger. "It's more than us they want, Your Highness. It's your whole world. They're from . . . a magical sort of otherworld. They want a stone of power that is found here. They call the stuff aafth. I don't know what you call it. It's common in your mines, but it's rare where these blue guys come from, and they can use its power to capture other worlds. They don't care how many people they have to kill to get it."

Beside me, Maggie shivered. "That's true. We saw them wipe out a whole village of your people. They just said, 'Natives get in the way.'"

Izor kept staring at the distant blue figures. His orange complexion suddenly turned pale. From anger, I guessed, not from fear. "So tell me, Josh the Oberon. How can my people be saved from these creatures?"

I thought a moment, then pulled the silver circlet out from my shirt. It popped back into its round shape, and I put it on my head. "This is the thing that will help them move the aafth from your world to theirs. We took it from them, and that's why they're following us."

"Then it should be destroyed to keep us all safe," Izor said.

Maggie squeaked, and I shook my head. "The problem with that, Prince, is that we need the circlet too. We can't get home without it."

"And," Maggie added, "the blue guys have got a sort of shiny staff thing that fits into the circlet. We can't leave without that either."

Izor's face lit up. "But I would be happy to have you stay. You would make my father's court far less boring."

I was honored and all. But there was no way I wanted to stay forever in this world, made-up or not. Writing about it was one thing. "That's very kind of you, Izor. But people get kind of attached to their homes. I mean, our parents are there and our friends and all."

"Yes, I see." His shoulders slumped a little. Then his expression hardened. "Well then, we must keep that circlet out of their hands and put the staff into yours."

Maggie frowned. "But the guards here just have bows and arrows. Can they keep the blue guys out? They've got pretty scary weapons."

Izor smiled proudly. "The temple walls are strong. And the followers of Nur are warrior priests. We will be safe here."

I hated to pop his bubble, but I wasn't feeling as confident. Walking across the room, I said, "But that bird was shot down by someone inside the temple." Grabbing the door handle, I yanked it. Nothing budged. "And the sneak Gom locked us in! He was Gorku's assistant. Maybe he doesn't like that you destroyed his master."

"Gom was Gorku's man?" the prince asked. "Even my father didn't know that. Your knowledge is indeed wonderful, Josh the Oberon."

"Yeah, well, my guess is that once Gom sees the blue guys, he'll thinks that it is *you* who they're after, since you're the prince and all. Maybe he'll try to sell you to them."

Maggie looked around the room. "Is there any way out of this room besides that door?"

Izor shrugged. "I've never been in this room before."

And I didn't write about it, I thought. "We could try the windows."

There were arched windows on two of the walls. Windows with no glass. We hurried over to the ones on the far side and scrambled onto the wide windowsills. I peered over and saw a narrow ledge running below the window. A very narrow ledge. Jagged rocks covered the ground several stories below.

I reeled back and tried to shake the dizziness out of my head. "That ledge is about as wide as a snail trail," I said. "And even if we don't fall, we don't know where it leads once it goes around the corner."

My shoulder itched. Suddenly Leggy ran down my arm and hopped onto the sill. The little guy looked back at me with a toothy grin. It hopped down to the ledge, skittered along, and vanished around the corner.

"Rats deserting a sinking ship," Maggie mumbled.

A loud boom shook the air and sent us rushing back to the other windows. We couldn't see whoever set off that boom outside the gate. But on the inside, a single purple-robed priest threw himself against a lever. *Gom!* Slowly, the gate opened.

"Treachery!" Izor cried. Maggie had already galloped back to the other windows and onto the window sill.

I swallowed. "Right. Let's split!" As I swung my legs over the edge, I tried not to look at the rocky teeth far below. Leggy peered around the corner and waved several pink and red legs. "Okay, pal," I muttered. "I guess I'd rather trust you than the guys in blue."

My feet didn't reach the ledge. I had to turn around and lower myself down, with my cheek scraping against the rough stone wall. Finally, my toes touched the ledge. Letting go of the windowsill, I jammed my fingers into grooves between the stones and began inching along. I pressed myself hard against the wall, but I could still feel the emptiness behind begging to drag me out and down.

I heard the others sliding out the window and following, but I didn't dare turn my head to look. The one moment when I forgot and looked down, a wave of dizziness nearly washed me off the ledge.

Finally, I edged around the corner. There was Leggy, scampering ahead of me to where the ledge met a tower a few yards away. I reached it and pulled myself through a wide slot in the battlements. My legs quivered like jelly as I dropped to the stone floor. I felt like kissing the broad, solid stones. I probably would have if Maggie hadn't joined me. She looked a little pale, but still bouncy. Izor arrived looking like he did that sort of thing every day.

The prince hurried to a small door in the stone wall of a round tower. "We must hide. Gom and your blue friends could be looking for us any moment." Maggie followed him through the dark doorway. I scooped up Leggy and did the same.

Wedge-shaped stone stairs spiraled down and down. The only light came through narrow slits in the wall. When those gave out, sputtering torches provided smoky light. I ran my hand along the outer wall, trying not to let dizziness take over. Like I'd said, the stones "felt fuzzy, covered with dark, dank mold." The stairs kept spiraling down.

Finally, my knees rattled. I realized we'd reached bottom. "We'll go through the Caverns of Nur," Izor whispered from the darkness ahead of me. "If those creatures are following us, we should lose them there."

That wasn't much comfort. I'd set a scene in the Caverns of Nur. They spread underneath much of the temple complex. But this was definitely not the sort of place you want to see outside of a book.

We shuffled forward. The passage was hot and stinky. I'd written that it smelled and felt a lot like Hell. Not that I'd actually been to Hell, but this was beginning to seem pretty close. The foggy darkness took on a red cast.

As Izor picked up the pace to a trot, Maggie whispered back to me, "Josh, do we really want to go in to these caverns?"

"No," I admitted. "But it's better than being melted by blue guys. Maybe. Keep going."

Our feet squelched through slippery gunk on the passage floor. I knew what it was and wished I didn't. Droppings, hundreds of years' worth. The sound disturbed bat-lizard things hanging from the ceiling. They filled the air in a squeaking cloud. I'd only mentioned them and their stinky droppings in passing to give a little detail to my scene. I hadn't mentioned their mouths full of needle-sharp teeth. As they zoomed past me, I cringed. Leggy didn't seem to mind. He stretched up, snatched one in his teeth, and began crunching it like a potato chip. Yuck.

The passage opened into a large cavern. It stank like a sewer, or like really old eggs. Torches lined the rough rock walls. Two large pools covered most of the cavern's floor. One pool held steaming, bubbling mud that occasionally shot up jets of flame. The other contained calm green water, "smooth, like a mirror." Narrow bridges spanned the pools.

Just ahead of me, Maggie studied the scene. *"This choice is pretty clear,"* she said, heading for the pool of emerald water.

"No!" Izor and I both yelled.

I picked up a stone and bowled it along the walkway where it drooped over the quiet pool. Instantly the water erupted. Leathery claws clamped onto the bridge, flicking the stone into a gaping mouth. "Didn't you read the book?"

Maggie had turned pale. "Guess I skimmed this part."

"Follow me," Izor called as he strode toward the other pool. "Carefully and quickly."

The mud pool bubbled and steamed underneath the narrow bridge. A jet of flame shot up on our left. Maggie and I flinched away, pinwheeling our arms so as not to fall off the other side. Flames shot up like fountains on both sides. In the lead, Izor moved smoothly along, but hey, he'd walked this before. I'd only written about it.

It was hard to see clearly through the clouds of stinky steam, but at least I could tell the bridge was arching down. Then I slipped on a splotch of hot mud. I flailed my arms but totally lost my balance. As I toppled over, I flung my arms around the narrow wooden span.

Hugging it like a monkey shinnying up a tree, I crept to the far end, then stumbled to my feet.

"Good work, bro!" Maggie cried, flinging herself into a staggering hug.

"Hush!" Izor hissed. "Let's hide behind these rocks and watch. Anyone following us should fall for that trap. Unless that traitor Gom is leading them."

"He's probably too cowardly to be in the lead," I said as we crouched behind a screen of tumbled rocks. "But don't count on fooling the blue guys. They've read the . . . I mean, they know things too. Probably didn't skim like *some* people."

Maggie stuck out her tongue at me. "So find someplace to run that's not in the book."

"How?" I whispered. "Everything I know about this world I wrote down."

Looking confused, the prince cleared his throat. "I know you are speaking of strange magical matters, but I do not understand . . ."

"I know," I apologized. "I'm sorry we keep talking about it! But I think you'd be a lot happier not understanding. . ."

"I've got it!" Maggie hopped up and, after a glance at Izor, pulled me aside. "Josh," she whispered. "That first draft you made me read—that was longer than the final book, wasn't it?"

"Lots. Miss Jordan said it was way too long. I didn't want to cut any of it, but the last Famous Author they brought in made a big point about how authors always have to cut and rewrite, so I . . ."

I slapped my forehead. I felt like hopping a bit myself. "Right! I get it. The blue guys probably only read the final version. I know stuff about this world that they don't."

After thinking a moment, I turned to the prince. "Izor, can you lead us from here to the High Sanctuary of Nur?" I hadn't described the route; I'd only said that Izor had taken it.

The prince turned pale. "To the door, yes, but I have never been inside. They say it is protected by powerful magic."

I smiled. "It is. But that's what Oberon and Puck are supposed to be good at—powerful magic."

CHAPTER SEVEN
USEFUL DETAILS

A wave of bat-lizards swept across the tunnel from the far side of the cavern. Peeking over our pile of rocks, I saw a white flash incinerate the hindmost bat-lizards. Quickly I scrunched down again. We were being followed all right.

Grating voices carried across the pools. One suddenly shouted, "No, fool! Did you not read the book?"

The answer was cut short by a horrible scream and a splash.

"Sounds like I'm not the only one who skims," Maggie whispered.

I tried to concentrate on my rather shaky plan. There was no way those guys could have seen the first draft. Was there? "Okay, Izor, time to get up and have you lead us out of here. Make sure the blue guys can see and follow us— but not too closely."

"Ah, you are planning some sort of trap." He smiled far more confidently than I felt.

We stood up and walked to the far cave wall. I glanced back to see two blue guys teetering across the bridge over the bubbling pool. Above the gurgling mud and swooshing fire jets we could hear their shouts. They must have seen us. Izor led us to the smallest of several doorways in the rocky wall. Once through it, he picked up speed, rushing up a steep flight of stairs. At the top, we burst into a large, book-lined room. A group of priests, quietly reading, jumped up and scattered like ants.

Dodging around tables, Izor dashed out a door on the far side and into a garden. We all slumped onto a stone bench to catch our breath. But not for long. Sounds from behind sent us jogging along flower-bordered paths, through a gate, and up the neat rows of an orchard. Hairy, grey, banana-like fruit hung from the trees and lay splattered on the ground. Again, I'd not bothered to mention that the fruit smelled like old fish. Maggie slipped on one of the fallen ones. I yanked her up from a pile of dripping, smelly grey gunk.

She glowered, but I just shrugged. "Hey, not my fault. I didn't really create these things."

The orchard ended at a plaza at the base of a mountainside. A large building stood on the mountain's peak. In the bright sunlight, its polished purple stone glowed, just as I'd described it, "like it had been sculpted from grape jelly." I was pleased with the description, but not with all the stairs I'd mentioned. They looked a lot more daunting in reality than they had in my mind. We climbed and climbed and climbed until we reached two great doors. They were dark wood, crossed by golden planks. And they were solidly closed. Black stone statues stood on either side of the doors, huge winged creatures that looked like flying lobsters.

"Those are statues of Nur, the mountain spirit," I whispered to Maggie.

She grunted. "Just the sort of weird thing you would dream up."

"Hey, I didn't . . ."

"I know, I know. You just tuned in. But this is just the sort of weird world you would tune in on."

"Great Oberon and Puck," Izor said. "This is as far as I can lead. Not even the crown prince knows the secret of entering here. But if you do, you had best use it now. The blue ones are not far behind."

I spun around. The two remaining blue guys wobbled up the stairs on their long noodley legs. Gom was well behind them now, purple robe hiked up over skinny orange legs. He grinned widely, preparing to take revenge on the prince.

Fear tingling through me, I turned back to the door. "Right. The door's magically locked. How did that incantation go? Something about rock and winds. Oh, yeah. 'Nur of the Rocks, Nur of the Winds, Nur of the blazing Sun and the glowing Moons, let us who seek your care enter into your abode.'"

Maggie grunted. "The lines are okay, but your delivery's lousy. No drama."

"Not everything's theater," I snorted. Turning to the

statue on the right, I twisted one of the lobster-thing's pincer-like hands. Silently, the great wooden doors swung open.

When I turned back to the prince, he was kneeling on the ground before me. "O most powerful, heroic and wise Oberon," he stammered. "Truly, your power—"

"No time for that now!" I shouted. I yanked Izor to his feet and pulled him inside. Maggie stepped inside after us. She gasped. "You cut this whole section out in your final draft?" she whispered. "It was my favorite part."

"Miss Jordan said it was way too long and gross. I really liked it, but out it went. Now I just hope that my first draft was just as tuned-in to this world as the second was. I'm counting on everything being the same."

I sighed and looked around. The large round chamber arched into a high ceiling. Torches around the walls made the purple stone glow like we were "in the heart of a gigantic jewel." I smiled. That was the same, anyway. Then I sneezed. I hadn't said anything about the air. It was filled with sharp, nose-tickling incense. The floor was covered in a chalkboard pattern of silver and gold.

In the center of the room stood three huge statues of Nur, carved from shining black stone. All as described, but a lot more impressive.

Deliberately leaving the door open, I trotted across the room until we came to the smallest of the three statues. "You can hide here, Your Highness. They aren't after you, just us. The trick is for us to get them where we want them, and for us to keep the circlet and grab the staff." A sigh seemed to wheel up from my toes. "I guess I'll have to . . ."

"Oh no you won't!" Maggie snatched the silver circlet and jammed it onto her own head. "This stunt calls for theatrics, and you can't act your way out of a paper bag."

I started to protest, but I had never seen Maggie more determined. "You know where to lead them?"

"Hey, I told you I *read* this part, and anyway. . . ." A shout from the doorway cut her short. Two tall, ragged rectangles stood silhouetted against the light. The leader strode forward, clutching the shiny staff.

"Infuriating creatures," it snarled. "You have led us on a pointless chase. But you cannot stop us. This vile world's wealth shall be ours. The galaxy shall be ours. Hand over the circlet now. Perhaps we shall spare some of this world's natives. Attached as you seem to be to the worthless scum."

Maggie suddenly leaped forward from behind a stone altar, arms raised. Torchlight glinted off the silver crown on her head. "Silence, great flatworms! You do not know worth when you see it. But I do. I am Puck, merry wanderer of the night!"

Crouching down, she threw back her head and howled out more of her lines from the play: "Up and down, up and down, I am feared in field and town. Goblin lead them up and down."

With a cry like an angry cat, Maggie began dancing wildly around the room. She took off her Flower Princess belt and cracked it like a whip. Clumsily, the two blue guys followed her, the lead one still clutching his nasty weapon.

I got down like a commando and scuttled along behind a row of offerings to the temple's fearsome god. Leggy squeaked with annoyance and scrambled from one of my shoulders to the other. I caught glimpses of my sister, and she was acting up a storm.

"Over hill, over dale," Maggie sang, cartwheeling over the floor. She jumped on a stone altar just as a flat blue arm grabbed for her, then deftly somersaulted off the other side.

"I do wander everywhere, swifter than the moon's sphere." She spun around and around back toward the center of the room, twirling her belt over her head. The blue guys stumbled after her.

I watched tensely, crouched behind the farthest of the three statues. In books, the heroes never seem to have doubts that their clever plans will work. I had plenty.

One of the blue guys lunged just as Maggie leapt off the ground and caught the lowest arm of the central statue of Nur. She scrambled up from arm to arm, continuing to chant Puck's lines.

Maggie grabbed the statue's snout and swung herself onto its back. Her two pursuers hopped about on the tiled floor below her. Obviously they were not climbers. Maggie waved her crown above them and intoned loudly, "I am sent with broom before, to sweep the dust behind the door!"

I watched the blue guys' feet. "More to the right," I whispered to myself. "More to the right."

My sweaty hand clutched the stone flower held in one of my statue's pincer hands. The blue guys leapt up. They missed Maggie's dangling feet, landing further to the right. Maggie leaned over, looping her belt toward the staff. It didn't reach far enough. She tried again, stretching farther, ready to fall at any second. Violently, I twisted the stone flower.

Just then I saw a swift movement: orange, not blue. "No, go back!" I yelled. Izor must have been shadowing the blue guys. He launched himself at them like a rocket. Snatching the staff, he tumbled to the floor, laughing triumphantly.

A grinding rumble drowned out his laughter. The stone floor in front of the statue dropped away, taking the shrieking blue guys with it. Screams echoed through the room—theirs and Izor's.

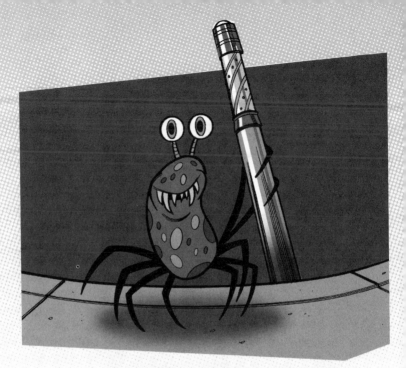

CHAPTER EIGHT
POWER OF THE PEN

I bolted from my hiding place. One of Izor's hands still scrabbled at the rim of the pit. Maggie dropped beside me and helped tug. When Izor was sprawled safely on the tiled floor, I gasped, "I'm sorry. We should have told you what we had in mind. About the secret pit, and the stuff they wouldn't know about."

Izor just shook his head. "I'm the one who is sorry. So very sorry. I lost hold of the staff. It's down there too."

I gulped. After a moment's silence, Maggie turned to me, her voice small. "What's down there anyway, Josh?"

"I don't know," I said. "I just said it was the secret pit where the evil High Priest Gorku dropped his sacrificial victims. No way we can go down after the staff."

Izor groaned. "Once again, I should have thought before I acted. I should have let you work your magic plan."

I sat beside him and patted his shoulder. "It was never much of a plan, really. And it was dumb of me to ask Prince Izor to just hide."

Maggie nodded glumly, "And anyway, you *did* grab the staff. I think my belt was really too short. That was really brave what you did, Izor."

I looked at her, then gave her an awkward hug. "That was brave what you did too. It was really some performance. I guess acting has more uses than I thought."

She shot me a wobbly grin. "Looks like writing does too. After all, I had good material—Shakespeare's words and your setting."

I nodded. "That last Famous Author was right. She said don't sweat about cutting stuff out of stories, because you can always use it somewhere else."

With a squeak, Leggy crawled out of my pocket. He chirped, then skipped down my arm, scrambled into the dark pit, and disappeared. "No, don't go!" I cried, but I grabbed for him too late.

I stared into the pit, trying not to think about how much it had stolen from me. Izor patted me on the back. "The dit-dit is probably happiest there. Caves and dark places are their natural homes."

"Home," Maggie said shakily. "Well, at least it's got one."

Prince Izor stood up. "And you two have as well. Josh the Oberon, Maggie the Puck. There is no way I can say how grateful the people of Yastol are to you and your strange magic. You will always have an honored home with us. I'm sure my father will . . ."

"Your Highness," a thin voice called from the doorway. We turned and saw the wizened High Priest hobbling our way through the opened door. "This is all very dreadful. I have just learned of those frightful creatures' incursion. The temple guards already have that faithless Gom under arrest. But it is unforgivable that anyone could loose such fiends against the crown prince of Jiz Tah!"

The prince walked to where the old priest stood. "There is nothing to be troubled over, Holy One. Wherever those blue fiends came from, they have been overcome by the strange magic of our two friends here. Two who are soon to become members of our court."

"Ah, yes, the court!" the old man piped. "Yes, yes, I must tell you. Your father and a troop of warriors are on their way. A message bird just arrived from the king. I am puzzled though, since I just learned that our bird was traitorously killed at the start of its voyage."

"My father was probably already looking for me. I'll wager he picked up my trail at the farm where I was working, or at the slavers' camp. How far is he?" Izor stopped and smiled as we heard a distant sound. "Not far, it seems. That sounds like royal trumpets."

We all rushed to the doorway. Beyond the towers of the temple complex, we could see a body of armed men winding their way up the mountain road. Royal banners whipped about in the hot, dry wind as trumpet notes again echoed among the purple peaks.

I watched them come, capes flying, armor flashing. The desert behind them stretched in shades of purple and pink until it faded into the pale lavender sky. There before me was all the glory and wonder of Yastol. As I had imagined it, as I'd thought I'd created it. But all I really wanted now was to see my very ordinary home, my messy room, and my non-royal parents.

I looked at Maggie, who was impatiently scrubbing tears from her cheeks. Together we turned to follow Prince Izor down the mountain.

"Ah, wait," squeaked the High Priest. "I need to close up the temple. I can't imagine how you made it past the safeguards, Great Oberon, but magic is magic, I suppose. Great merciful Nur! What is that?"

We spun around and stared past the priest into the temple. Legs, red ones with pink spots, were crawling out of the opening in the floor. Some of the legs waved a shiny staff.

"Leggy!" I cried, running back to meet the creature. "You're a bright little fellow!"

"Bright as they come," Maggie laughed. "And pretty too! Polka dots and all."

I took the staff and swept the dit-dit onto my shoulder. We rejoined the others at the temple door.

"Prince Izor," I said with a bow, "we don't want to seem ungrateful. Being part of your court would be great, but if we can make this thing work, I think we'll be heading home now." Then I grinned. "But somehow I don't see you just hanging around the court being bored. You're the kind of person who makes things happen. Maybe I'll keep in touch by writing . . . er, conjuring a sequel or something."

With a wistful smile, the prince said, "Who am I to understand the ways of magic workers? But I will miss you, Josh the Oberon and Maggie the Puck. Adventure is not the same without a dash of mystery and friendship."

After a bunch of hugs, I took the circlet and put it firmly on my head. "Okay, Maggie, I'll start thinking up a story about a brother and sister ready to walk home after rehearsing a play in the woods—on a world exactly like ours was yesterday. When I say the word, plug the staff into the three jewels on the circlet and hold on tight."

"Right."

I closed my eyes and tried to build up a picture in my mind, a picture with all the details. The damp smell of the woods, the raw feel of the early spring breeze, and all the birdsong—the cheery trilling of cardinals and the dreamy cooing of mourning doves.

"Make sure the two kids in the story remember all the adventures they just had," Maggie said.

I nodded. "Now!"

I felt like I'd been yanked inside out and back again. The glaring heat and harsh desert breeze were gone. I opened my eyes and saw the grey trunks and new green leaves of the woods in early spring, a woods on Earth. The cool breeze carried the rich smell of growing plants and the singing of birds.

"I like this ending a lot," Maggie sighed.

I took off the circlet and staff and put them in Maggie's hand. "Here, you can use these as play props. Whoever plays Oberon will look great in that crown."

"You don't want to use them again?" She sounded surprised—even a little disappointed.

"I don't think so. I guess I can blunder through that heroic adventure stuff if I have to. But it's not really my thing. If a world is exciting and dangerous enough to write about, I'd rather just do the writing."

I peeled off my translator net and handed it to Maggie as well. "But . . . eh . . . try not to break any of this stuff—just in case."

As we started walking home, Maggie said, "I bet I can guess what your entry in this year's writing contest will be about."

I laughed. "Maybe. But I don't have to worry about writer's block again. There's a whole universe of really strange things out there, just waiting to be written about."

"And not just there," Maggie said, pointing at my shoulder. I turned my head and grinned at the pink polka-dotted thing with all the legs and teeth, riding happily on my shoulder.

When I got to the fort, Maggie was already there.

I sat down, opened my backpack, and handed her a flashlight, a pocketknife, a walkie-talkie, and her translation hairnet. Then I pulled out the alien gizmo. Putting the crownlike silver circlet on my head underneath a translator net, I handed the high-tech staff to Maggie.

"Ready?" she said, grinning and waving the staff.

Suddenly I wanted to yell "No!" Scary memories from last time came rushing back. But I couldn't back out. During our first trip, Maggie got the idea that I was some sort of a hero. Like big brothers are supposed to be, I guess. Not a major wimp like I really am. It was a kind of cool change.

I took a big breath and grabbed Maggie's hand. "Ready."

I reached into my back pocket and looked over the finished draft of my story. I didn't want to mix up any details as I thought my way to the alien beach. My head jiggled as she jammed the edge of the staff into the circlet on my head. The sounds of birdsongs and rustling leaves suddenly cut out. All of the sudden, I felt like I was being turned inside out like a sweatshirt, shaken violently, and then yanked outside in again.

Sound came back: the soft hiss of waves on sand. Sun shone warmly on my eyelids. Slowly, I raised them. White sand sparkled into the distance. The air smelled fresh and tangy. An ocean stretched to the horizon, a brilliant blue green. I'd only been to the ocean once before when we'd visited an uncle. The skies had been gray then, and the water rough and cold. But the scene before me looked even better than one in any travel brochure. I'd done it!

Maggie let out a "whoop!" and ran down the beach where we stood. Feeling mighty pleased with myself, I sauntered down after her. The last doubt shuffled to the back of my mind. I should have made it stay front and center.

Skipping along the wet sand, Maggie laughed and threw rocks into the incoming waves. I looked down. Pretty pebbles dotted the beach. I'd said in my little story that a unicorn prince had been trying to collect more pretty rocks than anyone else. He stumbled into a hidden cave, where he found a mermaid princess with her tail caught between boulders. She'd given him the giant pearl she was wearing, and he'd freed her by prying the rocks away with his horn. Like Maggie said, a lame story, but it got us to the beach.

Maggie called out from the edge of the gently lapping waves. "OK, Josh. It's really nice here, but where are the mermaids? And the unicorns?"

"Hey, I only said the creatures lived on this planet. I didn't say where or how many. Just enjoy the beach, and maybe we'll see them later."

I enjoyed the beach, at least. I saw some really amazing seashells with points and spirals. And the beach rocks were even better than the stones my uncle and I had looked for. These rocks were clear, with swirls of red, purple, or gold.

I started picking some up, then remembered that I'd thrown an old marble bag into my pack for collecting stuff. I rummaged around until I found the bag. There were still a few special marbles in the bottom that I hadn't traded to a little kid down the block. I pocketed those ones and poured a handful of beach rocks into it.

"I just saw a mermaid maybe!" Maggie called. I looked up. Nothing broke the ocean's glassy surface.

"Maybe," I called as I reslung my pack and returned to rock hunting. "It could be dolphins or whales or that sort of thing. I didn't mention all the creatures this planet might have, just the ones you wanted."

In fact, I realized, *I didn't mention a lot of stuff.* I'd said there were forests beyond the sand, and there were. But I hadn't said anything about the purplish mountains beyond the woods or the even taller mountains curving up the coast. One peak had a little wisp of smoke trailing out of it. *A volcano?* I wondered. *Cool.*

There were sounds too that I hadn't written about. A pack of something like monkeys gibbered in the forest. Cawing birds skimmed over the waves. Like seagulls—no, more like flying snakes with seagull beaks. And then, the roar. A huge, hate-filled roar.

I spun around to look at the forest. Something big, black, and shaggy was stalking out of the trees. It roared again, baring gleaming white fangs. Maggie and I ran toward each other, colliding in a terrified hug.

"Th . . . think . . . think of another story!" Maggie stammered. But I couldn't think of anything except those teeth and . . . oh no . . . the single white horn jutting out of the beast's forehead.

"Maggie," I said, "I think that's one of your unicorns."

ABOUT THE AUTHOR

Pamela F. Service has written more than thirty books in the science fiction, fantasy, and nonfiction genres. After working as a history museum curator for many years in Indiana, she became the director of a museum in Eureka, California, where she lives with her husband and cats. She is also active in community theater, politics, and beachcombing.

ABOUT THE ILLUSTRATOR

Mike Gorman is a seasoned editorial illustrator whose work has been seen in the *New York Times, The New Yorker, Entertainment Weekly*, and other publications. He is also the illustrator of the Alien Agent series. He lives in Westbrook, Maine, with his wife, three children, a dog, a cat, two toads, and a gecko.